Slam Dunk Series

Zip, Zero, Zilch

Tess Eileen Kindig
Illustrated by Joe VanSeveren

D0064420

CPH.
SAINT LOUIS

For my Caitie, who listened, advised, and went to see the Globies with me

Slam Dunk Series

> *Sixth Man Switch*
>
> *Spider McGhee and the Hoopla*
>
> *Zip, Zero, Zilch*
>
> *Muggsy Makes an Assist*
>
> *Gimme an "A"!*
>
> *March Mania*
>
> *Double Whammy!*
>
> *Camp Bee-a-Champ*

All Scripture quotations, unless otherwise indicated, are taken from the HOLY BIBLE, NEW INTERNATIONAL VERSION®. NIV®. Copyright © 1973, 1978, 1984 by International Bible Society. Used by permission of Zondervan Publishing House. All rights reserved.

Copyright © 1999 Tess Eileen Kindig
Published by Concordia Publishing House
3558 S. Jefferson Avenue, St. Louis, MO 63118-3968
Manufactured in the United States of America

Library of Congress Cataloging-in-Publication Data
Kindig, Tess Eileen.
    Zip, zero, zilch/ Tess Eileen Kindig.
    p. cm. -- (Slam dunk seris)
    Summary: Hoping to earn enough money to go to see the Globetrotters basketball team, Mick agrees to babysit a rambunctious young girl, but it is his faith that gets him into the game.
    ISBN 0-570-07018-X
[1. Basketball--Fiction. 2.Babtsitters--Fiction. 3. Friendship--Fiction. 4.Christian life--Fiction.] I. Title.

PZ7+.K6663 Zi 2000
[Fic]--dc21
                                      99-046931

2 3 4 5 6 7 8 9 10 11   09 08 07 06 05 04 03 02 01 00

Contents

Bad Business

"Neeeeat!" my little sister Meggie squealed as my best friend Zack Zeno and I wedged his table hockey game through the front door. "Can I play with it?"

"Sure," Zack said, easing it up the stairs. "Do you even know what hockey is?"

Meggie scrambled up beside us. "Don't be silly! Course I do," she said. "It's what you play when you don't go to school."

Zack and I looked at each other and grinned. "That's not hockey!" we said at the exact same second. "That's *hooky*!"

Sometimes it's like Zack and I share the same brain. That's why I was so excited that he was moving in with our family for four months. His dad got laid off at the plant where he builds cars and won't be called back to work until April. The only job he could get until then is with the railroad. But working for the railroad means that he has to leave Ohio and go live in a motel in Minnesota. Zack doesn't have a mom at home. So it looked for awhile like he would have to move in with his aunt and uncle in Chicago. Lucky for us, my parents said he could come live at our house instead.

Two barking balls of fur shot past us up the steps and into my room. *Crash!* Something hit the floor with a thud.

"Muggsy! Piston! Knock it off!" I hollered at our dogs. Muggsy belongs to me and Piston belongs to Zack. We found them in the church parking lot a few weeks ago and adopted them. They're brothers and they're exactly alike—neither one listens to us.

Zack and I moved the hockey game around the corner of the hallway and into my room. My basketball lamp was tipped over on its side on the floor. As soon as I picked it up, the basketball fell off the base and rolled under the bed. Before I could get it, both dogs shot out the door and down the stairs.

"Hey, guys!" my dad hollered from the front hall. "Shut these animals in Meggie's room until we get done here, OK?"

We left the plastic basketball under the bed and ran downstairs. The front door was standing wide-open to make it easy to move Zack's stuff in. Both dogs careened around the front yard. Muggsy yanked one of Zack's T-shirts from a box and dragged it through the slushy snow. Zack grabbed the shirt and I grabbed Muggsy.

"Hi, Mickey!" a voice called. I looked up the street to see Trish Riley coming down the sidewalk from her house. Trish is a cheerleader for the Pinecrest Flying Eagles. That's the basketball team Zack and I play on. She's also my biggest fan. Take it from me—having a fan like Trish Riley is enough to turn your face the color of chicken pox—even if you're not a world-class blusher like I am.

"Hi, Trish!" I yelled, heading back to the house with my squirmy dog.

"Wait!" she hollered, breaking into a run.

My dad set down the box of books he was carrying. He tucked Muggsy and Piston under his arms and took them inside while Zack and I waited for Trish.

She crossed the yard holding a bright yellow envelope in one hand and one of her famous baseball caps in the other. She jammed the hat on her head and waved the envelope. "Guess what?" she called. "Sam Sherman's having a birthday party. Did you guys get invited?"

Zack and I looked at each other. "Nope," we said at the same time.

Trish tugged on the brim of her hat. It's this annoying thing she does whenever she talks to me. "Well, it's not for another week. Maybe he's going to give you yours at school. It's really going to be fun. His parents are taking everyone to see the Harlem Globetrotters."

Zack and I looked at each other again. The Harlem Globetrotters were so cool they left cool in the dust. Back before we made the rec department team we used to fool around trying to do tricks with the ball like they do. Of course now we're too busy learning the basics to worry about any fancy stuff.

What I wouldn't give to see the Globies in person though! But the odds of Sam Sherman inviting me to his birthday party are about the same as Michael Jordan inviting me to his party. Sam Sherman never lets me forget for a minute that I'm the shortest person in the entire fourth grade.

"Are you going?" I asked Trish. It kind of surprised me that he'd invited any girls.

"Wellll ..." She tugged on her hat again. "That depends on who else goes. The only girls who got invited were me, Brittany, and Kristy Shaw. Tony and Luis got asked. Oh, and LaMar. And those two guys Sam always hangs around with." She made a face.

I knew the guys she meant. Sam's buddies make my life miserable. No way would they want me going to the Globetrotters. And now that

Zack lived with me, they wouldn't want him going either.

"We probably won't get asked," I said. "But we don't care, do we, Zack?"

For a second Zack didn't answer. Then he said, "No, we don't care," and went over to the van to get another box.

He cared. I felt it like a punch in the stomach. I bent down and picked up the box of books my dad had left on the ground and headed for the house. Zack caught up with me at the door. He was carrying a box filled with stuff for Piston—his leash and his food and water dishes. We didn't say anything as we went upstairs. I knew we were both thinking how much fun it would be to watch the Globetrotters clown around.

"Where can I put my clothes?" Zack asked when he opened my closet door. "There's no room in here."

He was right. My closet looked like the first day of a garage sale. "I guess we're going to have to get rid of some of this junk," I answered as I knelt down and scooped up a bunch of old school papers off the floor. "You know, I was thinking …" I stopped to let an idea take shape in my head. "You and I could probably earn enough money to get our own Globetrotter tickets."

Zack picked up a fistful of loose pens and pencils. "Get real, Mick," he said. "There's no way! How would we earn that kind of money? Besides, your parents would have to buy a ticket for one of them to take us. And then there's parking and food ..." His voice wandered off.

I'd sort of forgotten about parking and food and the ticket for my dad. But there had to be some way to do it! We could start some kind of business—just until we got enough money for everything. But what kind of business? There hadn't been enough snow for a snow shoveling business. And it was way too cold for a lemonade stand. I fished a few marbles out of a dust bunny and thought. Nothing came to me.

Yip! Yip! Yip! A weird high-pitched bark whipped Zack and I around. My eyes popped. A little, tan, hairless dog was standing next to my bed barking at us!

"How did *you* get in here?" I asked the dog. It looked exactly like the Taco Bell dog on TV. Except that the Taco Bell dog speaks Spanish. This one didn't even speak English.

"Wow, this is wild!" Zack cried, crawling over to the dog. He tried to pet it, but it zipped under the bed.

"I'll bet he came in the front door and nobody saw him," I said. I got down on my hands and knees and looked under the bed. As soon as he saw me, the dog backed into the corner and let out another sharp bark.

"TACO! TACO! COME BACK, TACO!" somebody hollered. A skinny little girl crashed into my room. "WHAT DID YOU DO WITH MY DOG?" she demanded. She had the wildest, curliest hair I had ever seen growing out of a human head.

Zack and I stared at each other. We'd never seen this kid in our lives.

"Who are *you*?" I asked, ignoring her question.

"NEVER MIND!" she shouted. "I WANT MY DOG!"

"Is somebody here, Mickey?" Meggie called from her room. She cracked open her door and peeked out. "Who are you?" she asked the girl with the wild hair.

"I'M DULCIE ANN STEFFINS, AND I WANT MY DOG!"

"I'm Meggie," Meggie said, opening the door a little wider.

"NO! Keep the door closed!" I hollered.

Too late. Muggsy and Piston bolted out of Meggie's room and into mine barking like they were chasing a mail truck. Taco backed up on his skinny little legs and growled. Dulcie screamed. After that it was a dog explosion! Dogs raced across the bed. Dogs bounced off the walls. Dogs flew down the hall to my parents' room in a blur of fur.

"Stop!" I hollered, running after them. "Muggseeeeee!"

In the hallway I nearly collided with my dad and a bushy-haired woman I'd never seen before. "My daughter and her dog are wrecking your house!" the woman cried.

I would have agreed, but there wasn't time. I raced into Mom and Dad's room and caught Muggsy just as he was about to jump on the skinny, hairless dog. Dad grabbed Piston and the strange woman grabbed Taco. All three dogs struggled to get away. Dad and I raced to my room. We tossed our two in and slammed the door. That left the woman with the wild hair standing in the hallway trying to hang onto Taco.

"I'm really sorry about this," she said as Taco jabbed at her stomach with his back legs. "We're trying to move into the old Palmer house today. Across the street? But between Dulcie and Taco …"

Suddenly an idea blossomed in my head like a flower. A terrible idea. An idea I knew I'd be sorry for as soon as I said it. "Zack and I could watch Dulcie for you," I offered. "We run a babysitting business."

2

The Trouble
with Training

"We d-d-d-d-o?" Zack stammered. He looked at me like I'd just stepped off a space ship.

"Well, we're just starting one," I corrected myself. "We'd be happy to take care of Dulcie while you move. You'll have to take Taco back though."

I knew what Zack was thinking without him saying a word. He was thinking she ought to leave Taco here and take *Dulcie* back. I was thinking the same thing. But I knew Mom would never go for three dogs under one roof. Two were already pushing it.

The woman turned to Dad. "That would be wonderful," she said. "If it's OK with you."

Dad grinned at me. "Not a problem," he told her. I knew what he was thinking. Watching me and Zack babysit would be more fun than watching the Chicago Bulls.

"OK, so what do you want to do?" I asked Dulcie after her mother left.

She wrinkled up her nose and thought. "I'm a

handful, you know," she warned.

"A handful of what?" I asked, pretending not to get it.

For a second she looked surprised. Then she grinned. "I don't know. It's what my mom always says. I'm this many." She held up four fingers, changing the subject. She was the same age as Meggie.

"You want to go outside and watch me and Zack shoot hoops?" I asked her.

Dulcie shook her fuzzy head. "I want to play tea party," she said.

Meggie clapped her hands like it was the best idea since the invention of bubble gum. "Me too! I want to play tea party too," she cried.

Zack and I looked at each other and rolled our eyes. As much as we love the Globies, we do have our limits. And sitting around pretending to drink fake tea out of plastic cups the size of nutshells, was stretching them.

"You go have your tea party, and Zack and I will put Zack's stuff away," I offered.

Both girls shook their heads. "That's being a bad babysitter!" Dulcie informed us. She crossed her arms over her chest and glared at me. "And bad babysitters never get to watch me again."

That sounded pretty good to me. But then I thought of seeing Reggie "Regulator" Phillips tear up the basketball court, and I changed my mind.

"Let's go outside. We can ride bikes, OK?" I said quickly. As long as Zack and I put serious distance between us and those plastic teacups, what were a few spins up and down the street?

We headed outside with both girls in tow. I yanked open the garage door and pulled out Meggie's pink Big Wheel and an old rusty trike I used to have when I was little. "How are these?" I asked.

Dulcie didn't answer. She shoved her way around my dad's pickup to the back of the garage. "Get that out too," she said pointing to an old red wagon in the corner. "We can play circus train."

"What's circus train?" Meggie asked as I wedged the wagon out from behind Mom's yellow three-speed bike. "Do we get to wear costumes?"

"Of course," Dulcie answered. She jabbed her thumb toward the house. "Back inside, buddy," she ordered me.

I didn't much care for a four-year-old calling me "buddy," but I led the way back into the house. Mr. Zeno and my parents were sitting at the table having coffee. "How's it going?" Dad asked as we came through the side door into the kitchen.

I rolled my eyes. He chuckled and winked at me.

"I'm going to be a princess," Dulcie announced when we got up to Meggie's room. She clamped a cardboard princess crown over her wild hair. "And you can be a lion," she told Meggie. She grabbed a black Magic Marker from a box on the dresser and drew six crooked whiskers next to Meggie's mouth.

"Cool!" Meggie cried, looking at herself in the mirror. She growled and pounced on Zack, almost knocking him over.

"Whoa! Stop!" Zack cried, fending her off. "You're fierce. I get the picture. Let's go outside now." He shot me a I-hope-you're-happy-now look and headed for the stairs.

Dulcie stomped her foot. "No way, José!" she hollered after him. "You need a costume too. And so do you," she said, pointing a stubby, nail-bitten finger at me.

I ran into my room and came back with my basketball. "How's this?" I asked her. "I'm a basketball player."

"Mickey's a star!" Meggie agreed. She'd tied a bright red scarf to the belt of her jeans to make a lion's tail. She roared and clawed her hands in the air.

Dulcie shook her head. "There are no basketball players at the circus," she said firmly. "I want you to be a clown. You too," she said to Zack. "Two clowns."

"No way!" Zack told her. "NO WAY!"

I understood how he felt. We already looked like two clowns for having gotten into this mess.

Dulcie shook her head. "You're being BAD babysitters again," she warned us. "My mom said GOOD babysitters PLAY with you."

I looked over at Zack and shrugged. "What's it going to hurt?" I asked him. "It beats playing tea party, right?"

"Oh, all right," Zack whined. "Give me the rubber nose."

Dulcie handed over a pair of black plastic glasses with a huge pink rubber nose stuck on. Dad had gotten them at the church's New Year's Eve party last year. Then she turned to me. "Sit down," she ordered.

I sat on the edge of Meggie's bed and let Dulcie stare at me. She yanked my chin first one way, then the other. "You need red clown cheeks," she decided. She picked up a red Magic Marker and uncapped it.

"OH, NO, YOU DON'T!" I shouted, jumping up. "I draw the line at Magic Marker."

Zack laughed. "It sure beats tea parties," he reminded me. "Doesn't it?"

I sighed, sat back down, and let her draw. When she was done I had two red circles the size of quarters on my face. I also had a line at each corner of my mouth that swooped up like a smiley face. I looked at myself in the mirror and shook my head. I sure hoped we were getting paid a lot. We'd forgotten to tell Dulcie's mother how much we charged.

Outside, Dulcie made me get some rope from the garage. Then she made Zack tie the back of the wagon to the handlebars of the trike. And the back of the trike to the handlebars of the Big Wheel. Then she climbed on the Big Wheel and Meggie climbed on the trike.

"So, what are WE supposed to do?" I asked them, looking around. Now that we were actually outside, that fake tea was starting to look pretty good. "It's not safe for Zack and me to tie our big bikes to anything."

Dulcie laughed and patted her princess crown. "I already know that," she said. "Mickey, you get in the wagon 'cause you're the littlest and Zack can pull us."

My face turned pink as a petunia. It was bad enough when kids my own age made fun of my height. But when *preschoolers* did it, I wanted to make like a bear and hibernate. I looked around. Except for Dulcie's parents who waved and smiled from across the street, there was no one else in sight.

"OK," I agreed. My voice sounded as whiny as Zack's when he agreed to wear the rubber nose. I climbed into the wagon. My legs dangled over the sides and dragged on the ground. All I could do was tuck my knees under my chin and try not to think about how stupid I looked.

"OK, now, Zack, you pull us," Dulcie said happily. "But first we have to sing. We need loud music for the circus train."

"SING? Oh, no, you don't," I said, starting to climb out of the wagon.

Dulcie looked across the street. Her parents were unloading a table from the back of a truck. "MOM!" she bellowed. "Mickey won't play ..."

"OK, OK. What do you want to sing?" I sat back down.

Reggie the Regulator, Reggie the Regulator, Reggie the Regulator. Over and over I mumbled the name of my favorite Globetrotter in my head.

"The Flying Trapeze Song," Dulcie said. "LOUD!"

She opened her mouth and started to sing. She sounded like a crow with strep throat. I didn't know whether to laugh or join in. Before I could decide, Dulcie decided for me.

"SING, YOU BAD BABYSITTERS!" she

screeched. "SING!"

We sang.

Down Arvin Avenue we went—Zack pulling the wagon wearing his rubber nose. Me sitting folded like origami in the wagon. The princess and the lion pedaling furiously. And all of us bellowing "The Flying Trapeze Song" at the top of our lungs. I wondered if five dollars was too much to charge Dulcie's mother.

A car took the turn onto Arvin Avenue. It passed us, and then slowly backed up. I turned my head away and stared at the Polaski family's peeling yellow house like it was the most interesting thing on the planet. Slowly, the automatic window on the passenger side of the car buzzed down.

"Hey, guys!" Sam Sherman called. "Is this what you call basketball TRAIN-ing?"

3

Dulcie and the
Dumb De-fense

"Mickey! Zack's father is leaving now!" Mom called from the doorway as the Sherman family car made its way up the street again. A fluttery feeling, like tiny lizard feet, scampered across my stomach. In all the excitement of having Zack move in, I'd forgotten the sad side of today. Sam seeing the circus train was bad. But not as bad as what was about to happen.

Zack dropped the wagon handle and took off the glasses with the rubber nose. "I gotta go say goodbye," he mumbled, heading for the house.

I wasn't sure whether or not to follow him. "Want me to come too?" I called, climbing out of the wagon.

Zack shook his head no and kept going. I watched him climb the porch steps and disappear through the front door. I tried to imagine what it must feel like to be him, but I couldn't do it. It was impossible to think about being away from my family that long.

Dulcie grabbed my jacket by the elbow and

tugged. "Mickey! You're not listening to me!" she snapped. "Did you even hear what I said?"

"No," I admitted, still staring at the house.

"I SAID let's sing 'Pop Goes the Weasel' now," she whined. "You can pull the wagon until Zack comes back."

I picked up the handle of the rusty wagon and pulled it up the street. I sang "Pop Goes the Weasel," "My Country 'Tis of Thee," and "Itsy Bitsy Spider" as loud as a boom box. But inside I felt as dark and still as the sky right before a thunderstorm.

From the corner of the street I saw Zack's dad come out on the porch with my parents and get into his van. Then he pulled away and my parents went back inside. Zack never came out.

I wanted to go see if he was OK, but I couldn't leave the girls. So I just kept pulling them in the wagon and singing stupid songs until Dulcie's mother finally came to get her.

"This was so great!" Mrs. Steffins said. She shoved her bushy hair out of her face with the side of her arm and sighed. "Do you think you boys could babysit for me again tomorrow? Maybe for a couple of hours after school? It's been such a big help."

I started to say no. But then she reached into the pocket of her shirt and pulled out a crisp green

$5 bill. "Sure," I blurted. "The only nights we can't are Tuesday and Thursday. We have basketball practice then. And games on Saturday."

I knew Zack would explode when he heard what I'd signed us up for. But I could handle that easy. It was just like basketball. Before he could sink a bunch of protests, I'd play defense and remind him about the Globetrotters.

"Hey, Zack!" I hollered, storming through the front door of the house.

Dad looked up from the newspaper he was reading in his recliner chair in the living room. "He's upstairs, Mick," he said. "Mom's up there with him."

The lizard feet scampered across my stomach again. "Oh." For a second I stood at the bottom of the steps, not sure what to do.

"He's having a rough time right now," Dad added. "But he'll be OK. It's hard on him to be away from the only family he has. He really needs you to be a good buddy."

I nodded, but didn't say anything. I had never really thought about Zack feeling homesick. When he first found out his dad was leaving, it had been pretty bad. But once he knew he was coming to our house, it had been great. We'd made so many plans it would take us three years to do everything on the list. I knew it would be hard to say goodbye. I even knew he might cry and stuff. But what if he stayed sad forever?

Slowly, I climbed the stairs to my room. I heard Meggie come in from outside and start telling dad about the circus train. Upstairs it was quiet except for the soft sound of Mom's voice.

The door to my room was partway open. I stood in the hall and stared at it. It felt weird not being able to run in there like I always did. It was like it wasn't even mine anymore.

"I know it's hard, honey," Mom was saying to Zack. "You feel very lonely right now. I don't blame you for crying. I always cry too when somebody I love has to go away. But then I remind myself that it's only for a little while. And that wherever they go, God goes too."

Zack mumbled something, but I couldn't make it out. His voice sounded muffled like he was talking through a pillow. I felt sort of guilty for listening. And scared too. But what did I have to be scared about? My parents weren't going anywhere.

I tiptoed into the bathroom, shut the door, and sat on the edge of the bathtub. Whenever I feel this mixed-up, praying is about the only thing I know that does much good. Even if I don't get an answer right away, I always feel better knowing I shared it with Somebody Who cares.

The door to my room squeaked just as I said, "Amen." Somebody was coming out. I opened the bathroom door and saw Mom ready to go downstairs. She looked up and smiled when she saw me in the doorway. "I think Zack wants to be alone for a little while," she whispered. "Why don't you come down and peel some potatoes for me?"

The last thing on earth I wanted to do was peel potatoes, but I followed her to the kitchen. A pile of big brown potatoes stood by the sink waiting. I picked up the peeler and started hacking away at one.

I wondered how much Globetrotter tickets cost. If Dulcie's mom gave us another $5 tomorrow, we'd have ten. $10 seemed like it ought to buy one ticket. But it probably wouldn't even come close. The sudden, loud ring of the phone nearly sent me flying out of my sneakers.

Meggie raced into the kitchen and grabbed it before I could set down the potato. Lately, whenever the phone rings, she's like Superman—ready to leap over tall buildings in a single bound to get to it.

"He's peeling pertaters," she told the caller. "He can't talk now. Bye."

"WAIT!" I hollered, snatching the cord. Dirty potato water dripped down my arm and onto the white phone. I didn't stop to wipe it off. "I'm here!" I yelled into the receiver. "This is Mickey." I don't get all that many phone calls, so I didn't want to miss one. Especially if it was Sam inviting me to his party after all.

"Mickey?" a familiar voice asked. "That you? Coach Duffy here. There's been a change in the schedule this week. I'm calling practice for tomorrow instead of Tuesday."

"Oh, OK," I said. "We'll be there."

I hung up the phone, disappointed. No party invitation, only a problem. I'd told Dulcie's mom we would babysit. As much as we needed the money, there was nothing I could do, but tell her we couldn't do it after all. Basketball beat babysitting any day.

"Mom!" I hollered down the basement steps. "I need to go across the street for a second, OK?

Mom came upstairs carrying three cans of green beans. "Why? What's the matter?" she asked, lining them up on the counter.

I told her about Coach's call. And how I had told Mrs. Steffins I'd watch Dulcie. "So I'm just going to say I can't do it," I ended. "Basketball practice comes first."

Mom stuck one can of green beans on the magnet of the electric can opener and pushed down the blade. Both of us watched as the can whirred around in a circle, then stopped with a loud *thunk*.

"I don't know, Mickey," she said. "It seems to me like you took on a job and gave your word. Mrs. Steffins really needs the help right now. Her husband is going out of town on business tomorrow. I think you'd better offer to take Dulcie along to practice with you boys."

"But, Mom!" I wailed. "I can't do that! No way! The guys will laugh, and Zack will be mad at me. Can't you keep her here? She could play with Meggie."

Mom shook her head. "Sorry. Meggie and I both have dentist appointments." She laughed and ruffled my hair. "Don't worry. I'll make up a little goodie bag with treats and toys for her. She'll be fine."

She wouldn't be fine. She wouldn't be one bit fine. But there was no sense arguing. If her mother said it was OK, Dulcie was going to basketball practice with me and Zack.

I grabbed my jacket, clomped down the basement steps and out the side door. All the way across the street I prayed that Mrs. Steffins would tell me not to worry about it. That we could do it some other time. By the time she answered the door I was jumpier than a frog out of water.

Quickly, I told her that Coach had changed our

practice time, but that Dulcie could come with us to the rec center. "Of course, we understand if you don't want her walking to the park and back," I added, hopefully.

Mrs. Steffins laughed. "Mickey, you are the nicest boy! Most kids your age wouldn't think of those things. Dulcie would love watching you boys play ball. I'll tell her she has to be on her very best behavior."

My heart sank like a hook shot. I already knew Sam would bring up that stupid circus train tomorrow. That was bad enough. But when I showed up at basketball practice with a little kid— a little *girl* kid—he was going to have a field day. By the time he got done with me, I'd never live it down. I trudged home wishing I could hop a fast train to anywhere.

Zack was peeling potatoes when I walked into the kitchen. His eyes were as red as dragon eyes, but he looked better than I thought he would.

"Hey, did you hear the news?" I asked him, tossing my jacket on a chair. "We have to take Dulcie to basketball practice tomorrow." I know I'd planned on playing defense. But sometimes a good offense is the best defense. At least that's what I've heard.

"WHA-A-A-T?" Zack squawked, dropping the potato peeler in the metal sink. He whipped around and glared at me. "Are you crazy, Mick? What are you trying to do—get us run off the team?"

I opened my mouth and closed it again. To my amazement, Zack burst into tears, ran upstairs, and slammed the door to my room.

4

Baaaaa-d News

Coach Duffy shrilled his whistle. "Stop! Time out!" he hollered.

The whole Pinecrest team froze. Whenever Coach's cheeks puff out when he blows his whistle, we know he's not a happy man.

"Can somebody please tell me what's going on here today?" he barked. "That little girl over there could play better than you guys are playing." He pointed at Dulcie who was sitting in the bleachers eating dry cereal out of a plastic zipper bag and playing with a box of crayons. She looked up from her coloring book and grinned.

Sam Sherman caught my eye and pretended to open an imaginary umbrella. Ever since Zack and I showed up at practice with Dulcie he'd been on this Mary Poppins kick, pretending we were nannies.

"Knock it off, Sherman!" Coach hollered. "McGhee, what's the matter with you? You left Clemmons wide open out there."

A surge of heat shot up my neck. He was right.

I'd let Nick Clemmons make a clean break for the paint. No wonder he'd sunk a two-pointer easy. If this kept up, Saturday's game against the Brunswick Blue Dolphins was going to be a disaster. Our winning streak would be history.

And so would *my* winning streak. I wasn't even a starter and already I was a star. The last couple of games I'd scored buzzer-beaters that won the game. The local newspaper called me Spider McGhee. They said I'm so fast it's like I have eight legs. If I kept playing like this though they'd be changing it to *Snail* McGhee.

We went back to playing. Things only got worse. I tried to throw a three-pointer and missed. Anybody with half a brain about basketball would have known to pass. But not me. I had to try and be a big shot. By the time practice was over, Coach and I were not on the best of terms.

"Stay right there and don't move until we come back," I ordered Dulcie after he let us go. "Zack and I have to change."

"OK, Mickey," she agreed, fixing her blue eyes on me like I was some kind of museum display. I ignored it and followed Zack into the locker room.

"Well, if it isn't the nannies!" Sam Sherman called as we walked in. He took off one of his giant shoes and looked up at us. "Can I give you guys a little advice?"

"Knock it off, Sam," Zack said. He grabbed his gym bag and unzipped it.

Sam laughed. "Oh, I wasn't talking about you so much, Zeno," he said. "It's more your little buddy over there. Hey, Shrimpo," he said to me. "Next time you go into TRAIN-ing you might not want to CLOWN around so much. TRAIN-ing is serious stuff, you know." His voice was loud enough to be heard in Tasmania.

I knew I'd never live down that stupid circus train. If you looked at me in the right light, you could still see traces of yesterday's Magic Marker clown face. I stiffened, waiting for him to tell everybody exactly what he'd seen on Arvin Avenue.

"What kind of training?" LaMar asked from across the room. "You working out somewhere, Mick? Over at the Y?"

I shook my head no and waited again for the blast. Sam chuckled and yanked off his other shoe. "Oh, that's our little secret," he said with a grin. "Right, Shrimpo?"

I guess I should have been glad he didn't tell, but I was mad enough to explode. I pulled open my locker and grabbed my stuff. All I wanted to do was get Dulcie, and get outside. I needed cold air like a starving guy needs pizza.

"Meet me in front of the building," I said to Zack, not waiting for an answer.

I hadn't changed out of my uniform, but I didn't care. I figured I'd throw my jeans on over the shorts. All I wanted to do was leave without talking to anybody. I kept my eyes open for Coach. He was nowhere around. Quickly, I slipped into the gym and over to the bleachers where I'd left Dulcie. She'd better not give me any trouble, I thought. She'd better just pack up her stuff, put on her jacket, and ...

She was gone!

I stared at the bleachers, my heart thundering. "Dulcie!" I hollered. "Where are you? This isn't funny, kiddo!" (Kiddo is what my dad says whenever he starts getting mad at me or Meggie.) I was so scared I could hardly breathe.

"DULCIEEEEEEEE!" My voice echoed in the empty gym.

"What's wrong?" Zack burst through the door, his eyes wide. "Don't tell me she took off!" He groaned and slapped his forehead with his palm. "We're in deep trouble now, Mick," he said.

Like I didn't know it. I ignored him and ran around behind the bleachers. No Dulcie. I looked underneath. No Dulcie there either. Every news story I ever have seen about missing kids flashed through my mind. "You run outside and look," I said to Zack. "I'm going to search the hall."

Tears burned my eyes as I ran to the snack bar. *Please God, help me. Help me!*

"Dulcie Ann Steffins, you get out here right now!" I hollered.

Silence.

I pivoted and ran back toward the gym. Then I thought of the locker room and ran the other way again. I yanked open the door and stuck my head in. "You guys see that little kid who was with me before?" I called.

Sam Sherman was combing his hair in the mirror. He turned around and started to say something. The look on my face stopped him cold.

"She hasn't been in here," Tony said. "Want us to help you look for her?"

I didn't take time to answer. If Dulcie didn't show up in the next few minutes, I would self-destruct. All that would be left of me would be a few teeth and the piece of stick-up hair on top of my head.

Zack ran in from outside just as I got to the front lobby. "She's not there, Mick," he said, panting. "I ran clear over to the pool house and through the parking lot. She's nowhere."

"Oh, man! We've gotta find her, Zack!" I cried. "We've GOT to!" I didn't even swipe at the tears that were leaking out of the sides of my eyes. All I could see was Mrs. Steffins' face when I told her Dulcie was lost.

The door to the kitchen swung open and Coach Duffy came out. "Time to go, boys. We need to lock up for the night," he said.

I swung around and looked at him. "Coach, we need your help," I cried. "That little girl we brought is gone!"

"Gone? What do you mean...gone? You've looked around? How can she be gone?" For a second Coach Duffy's wide forehead wrinkled. Then he took a hard look at Zack's wild eyes and my tears and snapped into gear.

"OK, quick! Fan out and make one last run of the place. If she's really not here we need to call 9–1–1. Go on—move!" he commanded.

Zack rushed through the doors to the parking lot. I headed for the locker room. My breath was coming in hard, jagged spurts. *Please God. Don't let anything happen to her. She's just a little kid. Please God. Please God.*

I passed the restrooms and skidded to a halt. The restrooms! Why hadn't I thought of them before?

I ran back and pulled open the door to the men's room. Dulcie couldn't read. She wouldn't know which bathroom was which. "Dulcie!" I called. "You in there?"

No answer.

I ran to the room marked *Women*. My hand froze on the door handle. It felt weird opening it. I knew there were no girls around today. Not even any of the moms had come in from the parking lot. This was an emergency—a *serious* emergency! I jerked it open a quick inch and looked away. I needed to shout inside if Dulcie was going to hear me. There was no choice—I had to look.

"Dulcie!" I yelled through the opening. All I could see was a wall of yellow tile. I eased the door open another inch.

Maybe we were going about this all wrong, I thought. Maybe she'd heard us screaming and got scared and hid. Maybe we should try to sound normal. A weird kind of calm came over me. Only God could have made *that* happen, because I was way too scared to do it for myself.

"It's time to go now, Dulcie!" I called in a friendly voice. "Let's get moving, OK?"

No answer.

"She's not here!" I hollered, tearing back down the hall to the lobby.

Coach, Zack, Sam, Tony, LaMar, and a couple of other guys from the team stood in a huddle by the front doors. They looked up when they saw me coming. "I'm calling 9–1–1," Coach said. He pulled a cell phone out of his shirt pocket and dialed the numbers.

Calling 9–1–1 meant it was real. Dulcie was really gone. And Zack and I were going to have to tell her mom.

I looked at Zack. He stared back at me. His eyes were as round and scared as a trapped rabbit's. Coach talked for a few seconds. Then he pressed a button and got off the phone.

"The police will be here in a few minutes," he said. "Everybody but Zack and Mickey go straight home. Now! No hanging around, you hear me? The police will take care of it." He shooed the team through the front doors. Tony and LaMar both looked back like they wished they could stay and help.

I had stopped crying, but I was shivering. It had nothing to do with the door opening and closing either. With everyone gone, the rec center seemed huge and alien. Coach Duffy flipped on the outside lights even though it wasn't dark yet. "You boys stay here," he said. "I'm going to take one last look by the pool house." He shoved open the door and left us staring out at the parking lot. The sky was the color of old gym socks.

"We gotta pray, Mick," Zack said when Coach was gone. "Now."

I nodded and closed my eyes. I could feel Zack put his hand on my arm. His fingers were icicles against my skin. "God, please help us find Dulcie," I whispered. "In the Bible it says that if a guy has a hundred sheep and one of them's missing, he should leave the 99 and go after the lost one. We're trying to find one of your lost sheep right now. The one named Dulcie Ann Steffins. Please keep her safe and show us where to look and ..." My eyes flew open.

A green and white police car roared to a stop in front of the rec center.

5

A Bright Spot of Yellow

A policeman with arms as big as telephone poles got out of the car just as Coach Duffy came around the side of the pool house. From inside the rec center we could hear the static of his police radio.

"You the guy who called 9–1–1?" he called to Coach.

Coach nodded and jogged over to the cruiser. Zack and I stood at the door and watched them talk. By the time they came in, I was practically jumping out of my basketball shoes. Zack described Dulcie's fuzzy hair and her pink high-top sneakers. I explained how we'd had to take her to practice. AND how she'd promised to wait in the bleachers.

"You sure you boys checked this place out good?" the policeman asked when we were done.

We nodded.

"You see any strangers in here—anybody suspicious?"

We shook our heads no.

"Was there anybody here the little girl knew? Somebody she might have felt safe leaving with?"

Again, we shook our heads no. "She only knows us. She just moved to this neighborhood this week," I offered. "Can't we just go look for her?"

The policeman ignored me and turned to Coach. "Did you see every member of the team leave the building?" he asked him.

Coach wrinkled his forehead and thought. "Well, no," he admitted. "I saw most of them. But I guess there were a few who left while I was back in the kitchen."

"I'll need their names," the policeman said shortly. "Everybody stay here. I'll be right back." He pushed open the door, got back in the cruiser, and said something on his radio.

Zack and I stood at the door and watched. Coach went behind the snack bar and came back with a pen and notebook.

"Who left early?" he asked, more to himself than to us. "Uh, Roberts and ..."

It all seemed so unreal, like we were actors in a scary movie. I didn't think it was our fault. But it probably didn't matter. We were the ones responsible for her. I looked over at Zack. He kept staring out at the police car. What a great start to our four-month sleepover this was! I wished I'd thought of a dog-watching business instead of a kid-watching business. A weird, squeaky sound snapped my attention back to the rec center.

"Did you guys hear that?" I asked. My voice sounded loud in the empty lobby.

"Hear what?" Zack asked, still staring at the cruiser.

Coach put down his pen. "I think I did hear something. Wait! Listen!"

We strained our ears. There it was again—a high-pitched sound like a yelp.

I jumped up and ran for the gym doors with Zack and Coach right behind me. "Dulcie! Is that you?" I called, pulling on the door handle. Even before I got the door open I knew it was. She was making the same kind of noise my dog Muggsy had made when we found him in the church parking lot after he'd been run over by a car.

"YOU BAD BABYSITTERS!" she wailed when she saw us. "Where were you? Why did you leave me here?" She was clutching the zipper bag of cereal with both fists.

For a second I could only stare at her. She was sitting in the bleachers exactly where I had left her!

"Where were you when it was time to leave, Dulcie?" Zack demanded as he and Coach came up behind me. "We came out of the locker room and you were gone."

Dulcie shuddered and let out another wail. "I had to go to the bathroom!" she cried. "But I came right back. And I stayed in the bleachers, just like you said."

"Didn't you hear everyone calling you?" Coach asked, shaking his head.

Dulcie wiped her nose on the sleeve of her shirt. "Yes," she said, sniffling. "And I called 'I'm heeeeere, Mickey,' but nobody answered. I only did what you said."

My knees felt as mushy as mashed potatoes. "Get your stuff and let's go," I snapped, grabbing her jacket and the bag my mom had used for the treats.

"You don't have to be so mean, Mickey," she whined. "You guys are the ones who messed up. I'm only this many." She held up four fingers and sniffed loudly.

"You're blaming US?" Zack cried. "When you're the one ..."

"Hey, that's enough. Everybody settle down," Coach said. "This is no time ..."

The gym doors opened and the policeman stuck his head in. "I need you all back out in the ..." He stopped when he saw Dulcie. "Oh, I see you found her." He came over to the bleachers. "Didn't anybody think to look in here before?"

"We looked," I told him. "She wasn't in here then." I didn't say we'd only looked once. I think he already thought we were the dumbest people on the planet.

The policeman sighed and motioned for Coach to follow him. They went over by the scoreboard to talk. I jammed Dulcie's crayons in their box and Zack shoved the coloring book in the goodie bag. We were stuffing her arms in her jacket when the policeman came back. "OK, kids, come on," he said. "I'll give you a ride home."

"NO!" I cried. "I mean, no thank you, sir. We can walk." The last thing I wanted to risk was somebody seeing me pull onto Arvin Avenue in the backseat of a police car.

But he hadn't been making an offer. "Oh, no, you don't," he said. "Into the car."

We had no choice. We piled into the backseat of the cruiser. Dulcie sat in the middle, and Zack and I sat on each side staring out the windows. Zack and I didn't want to talk. But now that she was safe, Dulcie chattered like a wind-up toy.

"I thought you were supposed to be good basketball players," she said as we pulled out of the rec center parking lot. "I don't think you're good. I think you're very bad. Very bad basketball players. And very bad babysitters. And I'm going to tell my mom."

I gritted my teeth and didn't say anything. Neither did Zack. All I wanted to do was get home and get something good to eat. Like macaroni and cheese from the box. Or a fried baloney sandwich. Compared to babysitting, basketball was a game for sissies.

It was just starting to get dark as we turned onto Arvin Avenue. The minute we pulled in the driveway, Mom ran out on the porch. "Mickey! Honey! What happened? Thank God you're safe. I was just beginning to get worried," she cried as we climbed out of the cruiser.

She ran down the porch steps toward us. Across the street at the old Palmer house the porch light flipped on. I held my breath as the door opened and Dulcie's mom came out.

"Honest, Mom, we did everything we were supposed to ..." I began.

"If she had just stayed in the bleachers like we told her ..." Zack added.

"That's right, if she ..."

Our words tumbled over each other like acrobats. By the time Mrs. Steffins made it across the street, Mom looked confused.

"Evenin', ma'am," the policeman greeted Dulcie's mom. "This your little girl?"

Mrs. Steffins nodded her bushy head. She'd run outside without her coat and was hugging herself in the cold wind.

"Just a little mix-up," he assured her. "Nothing to worry about. But I think it might be better if these boys did their babysitting a little closer to home from now on."

My face turned the color of the rusty trike from the circus train. He was making it sound like it was all our fault! And it could have happened to anybody! I bit my lip and stared at the ground. Mrs. Steffins swooped down and picked up Dulcie while he filled her in on what had happened. It was like Zack and I didn't exist. She thanked the policeman and hurried across the street without even saying goodbye. Dulcie made a face at us over her mother's shoulder. I wanted to make one back, but didn't.

"OK, then, I'll be off," the policeman said to Mom. "You boys did OK," he told us. "But in the future—don't mix basketball with babysitting, OK?" He gave us a crooked grin and got in the cruiser.

As soon as he pulled out of the driveway, Meggie shot out of the front door. "I don't want you to go to jail, Mickey!" she cried, tackling me around the knees.

"Nobody's going to jail," Mom said, peeling her off me. "Mickey didn't do anything wrong."

"I blame myself for asking you boys to take her

with you," she said to Zack and me as we went inside. "I should have known better. I'm really sorry, guys."

"It's OK," I mumbled. I like having the kind of mom who says she's sorry when she's wrong. I'm just never sure what I'm supposed to say back. It's sort of embarrassing.

Muggsy and Piston raced past us up the stairs and Meggie followed. All of a sudden, I was glad to be home. I didn't even care that we probably wouldn't get paid. Dulcie was safe and Mom knew we'd done the best we could. From the smell of things we were also having meatloaf for supper. *Thank you God*, I thought as I followed Zack around the corner of the landing.

"Hey, wait 'til you taste my mom's meatloaf," I told him. "It's got like half a bottle of ketchup baked on top. I'm so hungry I could eat a ..."

Before I could say "horse," I saw it. A bright yellow envelope poking out of the back pocket of Zack's jeans.

Six Steps to Lonely

I knew what it was. It was the exact same envelope Trish had been waving the day she'd told us about Sam Sherman's birthday party.

"Hey, what's that in your pocket?" I asked, trying to sound casual.

We went into my room and Zack flipped on the light. Right away I spotted the sleeve of my State T-shirt sticking out from under the bed. Whenever something turns up missing in the wash my dad always blames it on these made-up little people. He calls them the House Grabbies. I'd thought the House Grabbies had gotten my T-shirt for sure.

Zack flopped down on the lower bunk. "Just Sam's invitation," he said, yawning. "It's the same as yours. Man, am I tired!"

There was just one problem. I didn't *have* an invitation. I got down on the floor and made a big deal out of getting my T-shirt. While my head was still under the bed, I said, "You going? I still think we can get our own tickets to the game." I held my breath and crawled under farther to get the plastic basketball that had fallen off my lamp the other day.

"Yeah, sure," Zack said above my head. "Why not? Yeah, I'm going. This babysitting thing's not working out too great."

He was sure right about that. I grabbed the ball and crawled out backwards, bumping my head on the side rails of the bed. I got up and leaned my elbows on the mattress. "Yeah, babysitting is not the business for us," I agreed. "I was thinking maybe we could switch. Start something else. How do you feel about a paper route?"

Zack propped himself up on one elbow and looked at me like I'd just suggested we take up plumbing. "No way, man!" he groaned. "You have to get up at like 5:00 in the morning. Even when it's freezing. Uhh-uhh. I say we just give up and go to the party."

I didn't answer right away. I didn't want to admit I hadn't been invited. But even more, I didn't want to hear him say he was going without me. To buy some time, I started looking for the Krazy Glue to put the basketball back on my lamp.

"Don't you think we should go?" Zack asked. "It'll be fun. That Globie is too cool."

He was right. The Globetrotters' mascot, Globie, is really funny. Especially when he dances with the fans in his high-top sneakers. "I didn't get invited," I mumbled. I spotted the tube of glue on the windowsill and went over to get it.

Zack sat up. "Whaaaat? There has to be some mistake. I got my invitation at practice."

"Well, I didn't," I said, my back to him. "And I'm not going to. You can still go if you want. It doesn't matter to me. I'm going to earn the money and go with my dad." I swallowed hard and picked some lint off the top of the Krazy Glue cap.

Zack didn't say anything for what seemed like forever. Finally he swung his legs on the floor and sat up on the edge of the bed. He said, "Look, Mick, if you aren't going, I'm not going. It wouldn't be right."

I turned around and looked at him. The slump of his shoulders was like a billboard with huge, screaming, red letters. He really wanted to go to the party. Either he didn't think we could get the money to go ourselves, or, worse yet, he didn't want to go with me.

"Mickey! Zack! Dinner, guys!" Mom called from the foot of the stairs.

"Hey, it doesn't matter. Really. I want you to go," I told him. I took a deep sniff of dinner and sighed. "Come on—that meatloaf's calling us." But my throat was so tight I couldn't have forced ice cream down it. Not even Cookies N' Cream, my favorite.

After dinner, Zack and I cleared the table. We hadn't said anything else about the party. I headed for the kitchen with a stack of plates just as the doorbell rang. "I'll get it!" I hollered.

I set the dishes on the counter and dashed into the living room. Mom was already at the door. She opened it and snapped on the porch light.

"Linda!" she cried. "Come in."

I backed away. Linda was Mrs. Steffins. I figured she was here to yell at us for almost losing her kid. I heard her say something about needing to get right home, so I made a beeline for the kitchen.

"Dulcie's mom," I whispered to Zack.

He closed his eyes and scrunched up his face. I knew just how he felt.

Pretty soon the front door closed and Mom came into the kitchen. She was smiling. "Hey, guys, good news." She held up a $10 bill. "Mrs. Steffins said to give you this. She's sorry for all the trouble and says she understands what happened. She was too upset to deal with it before. She also wants to know if you'll watch Dulcie on Saturday after your game. At her house this time. I told her you'd call."

Zack and I exchanged looks. He shook his head

no, but I jumped in. "Sure, we'll do it. At least I will," I said quickly.

Zack didn't say anything. I swatted him with the dishtowel. "Hey, you in or not?" I asked, grinning.

"Not," he mumbled, staring at the floor.

I felt myself go numb. He was going to Sam's party without me. He didn't need to babysit because he didn't need a ticket. After we finished up in the kitchen, I went up to my room and left Zack downstairs watching TV with my parents. It felt good to be alone in my own room with my own dog. I did my math—well, *most* of my math—and glued my lamp. After that I moped around and thought about the Globetrotters. When Zack came up for bed, I changed into my pajamas and went downstairs.

"Hi, sweetie," Mom said, looking up from her sewing. She always does craft stuff in the evening. Right now she's making a picture of birds on a beach made out of zillions of tiny thread "x's." It looks very boring just pulling thread up and down, but she likes it.

"Hi," I mumbled, flopping down on the couch beside her.

"Something wrong?" She looked up over the little half-glasses she wears to sew.

"Yeah. I mean no." I stared at the TV. Mom

and Dad were watching a show about a rich doctor who lives with his dad and a dog named Eddie. It's boring too. I sighed as hard as I could and crossed my arms over my chest. I wanted her to see just how miserable I was without actually having to say it.

"Would this be about Sam's party by any chance?" She poked her needle into one of the little holes in her cloth.

"Sorta," I said. Zack must have told her that he got an invitation and I didn't. I looked over at my dad. He was watching the screen and laughing at Eddie, the dog.

"I told Zack he could go without me," I said. That was her cue to tell me what a great kid I was. And how she would never let that happen because it wouldn't be fair to me. I should have known better though. My mom hardly ever gets cues. If she were an actress in Hollywood, she'd get fired for missing so many cues.

"Oh, Mickey, that's so generous of you," she said. "Zack really needs this party right now. Poor little guy, he's so sad."

She put down her sewing and smoothed down the stick-up hair on the top of my head. "I know it's hard, honey. Sometimes the hardest thing in the world is to choose to be kind. Especially when you're hurt. But loving our neighbor is one of the most important things God asks us to do."

I didn't want to hear what else was coming. "Yeah, I know. G'night, Mom," I said, giving her a quick kiss. I said goodnight to Dad and headed for the stairs.

I knew Mom was right about God and love and all that. But right now, I felt too crummy to listen. Ever since his dad left, it was like Zack was the most important person in the world. Sure he has feelings. But what about my feelings? When was I going to get to be the neighbor everybody was supposed to love?

I trudged up to my room, hoping Zack was asleep.

No such luck. He was sprawled on the bottom bunk reading a basketball book from the school library. It was the very same book I've wanted to read for a whole month. He'd seen it first and I'd told him to take it. "Hi," he said, looking up.

"Hi," I answered, not looking at him. I felt like grabbing the book out of his hands and tossing it on my bunk. I opened my dresser drawer and started hunting for a clean shirt for school tomorrow. He must have known I was mad because he didn't say anything else and neither did I. Pretty soon the silence turned into a big, ugly, black thing that took up half the room and gobbled up all of the air.

"Mick?"

"What?" I yanked a striped shirt by its sleeve from the drawer. My voice had an edge as sharp as the rim of a rusty tin can.

"I heard that the Globetrotters are only going to be at the high school," he said. "Not at Gund Arena. So the tickets are way cheaper. Only $15 each and parking is free. Food will be way cheaper too. Which means you won't need as much money."

The ugly black thing high-tailed it out of my room. "Really? Wow! That's great!" I cried. "We've got $15 already—that's one ticket. And the babysitting job on Saturday will give us $5 more. I bet if we could nail down another $10, my dad would be able to take care of everything else. We're there, buddy!"

I started to go over to high-five him, but stopped before I took the six steps to the bunk. I'd just realized something. He hadn't said "*we* won't need as much money," he'd said "*you* won't." The difference between "you" and "we" is huge. A whole lot wider than six steps.

7

Natural Disaster

I could feel the rumble under my feet. There was going to be an earthquake. The Brunswick Blue Dolphins were going to shake the game wide open. At ten minutes into the first half we were running neck and neck. But all that was about to change. And some big hulk of a kid named George was the guy who was going to change it.

George is a Blue Dolphin turbo-charger. I'd heard rumors about him, but I'd never seen him before Saturday's game. I sat on the bench and watched him chest-bump his way down the court past Tony and LaMar. He was like one of those trick snakes that spring out of a can when you take the lid off. In nine minutes flat, he'd forced two turnovers and scored six points from layups.

Our guys gave it all they had. Tony saw a chance for a rebound and dove. He hit the floor with a thud loud enough to be heard in China. For a second he lay there dazed. Then he let out a moan that made me flinch. The game stopped and Coach Duffy rushed out on the court. He and the ref helped Tony up and walked him back to the bench.

Coach gave me the nod to take his place. Just like that, I was in the game! I'm sixth man, but this was the first time I'd ever played in the first half. I was sorry Tony got hurt. But I'd been waiting all season for a chance like this. I'd show those Blue Dolphins how basketball ought to be played! I blasted onto the court and took possession of the ball.

"Gimme an M! Gimme an I! Gimme a C! Gimme a K-E-Y! GO-OOOOO, MICKEY!" Trish Riley screamed. She turned three handsprings and landed in the splits.

Right away, George the Giant danced in front of me so close I could smell his sweat. I pivoted right. Left. Right again. I was in the three-point zone. I knew I should pass. LaMar was right there waiting for me to do it. But I couldn't. Who knew how long I'd be in the game? If Tony's shoulder felt better I'd be out. I had to go for it. I *had* to! I was a star! I threw and …

Missed.

The fans groaned. I zoomed in for a rebound. Too late. Zack scuffled, got it, nailed it.

The crowd roared its approval.

Like a pack of wild dogs, we all ran to the other end of the court. I saw a chance to go for a steal.

But before I could grab it, George the Giant lumbered in front of me like a gorilla. Quick as lightning, I ran first one way. Then the other. Then back. Then the same way again. George must not have heard about my famous Spider Strategy. I faked him out and made it to the paint. Another Dolphin had grabbed the ball while I was trying to hold off the giant. He aimed and let it fly. Without thinking, I jumped for it. And knocked it to the ground.

The ref's whistle blew.

"Personal foul on Number 11, Mickey "Spider" McGhee!"

The words blaring over the microphone turned me redder than the sauce on a chili dog. I knew better than to mess around with a shot that was already in the air. Now the Dolphins got to step up to the free throw line. Their guy easily sank both shots.

At halftime Coach Duffy cornered me in the locker room. I pretty much knew what was coming. "What were you trying to do out there?" he demanded. "Basketball is a TEAM sport, McGhee. Remember that, or you can stay on the bench."

I stared at the ground and mumbled, "Yes, sir."

I know it's a team sport. And most of the time I'm a team player. But it was like I didn't care today. I felt reckless and revved up. The minute I stepped on the court I'd felt it. And even missing the three-pointer hadn't knocked it out of me.

Tony's shoulder still hurt at the start of the third quarter, so Coach let me go back in. I knew he didn't want to, but I was the best he had.

Focus, Focus, I told myself. For a second I felt like maybe I could. But as soon as the action heated up, I lost it again. The Dolphins copped a steal and landed a two-pointer. I was all over the court, with George the Giant right behind me playing a mean man-to-man defense.

Near the end of the third quarter, a Dolphin got fouled for trying to grab the ball while I had it. I stepped up to the foul line and missed both shots. Then Sam Sherman missed a layup and LaMar got zapped for traveling. It wasn't until the fourth quarter that Pinecrest finally got back into the game. And it was Zack who took us there. He whipped out a whopper of a shot.

From the three-point zone.

With one hand.

The crowd flew to its feet.

"ZACK! ZACK! HE'S OUR MAN!" the cheerleaders screamed. "IF HE CAN'T DO IT, NO ONE CAN!"

I know it's just a cheer. They say it a lot. They've said it for me. But when I heard them say that nobody could score like Zack, my blood raced. It was like my veins were the speedway and today was the Indy 500. I muscled my way down the court through a knot of Dolphins who weren't paying attention. I wanted that ball. *Bad.* And I wanted it NOW!

A Dolphin shot and missed. Zack grabbed it on the rebound and sank it. We dashed to the opposite basket behind a tall skinny Dolphin who was dribbling like a maniac. He shot. Missed. Zack grabbed the ball and tried to sink it. But George the Giant blocked him and he passed to LaMar. LaMar missed the pass. A Dolphin got possession and passed to a red-haired kid who passed it to Giant George. The giant took off. I pounded after him. Darting around a Dolphin guard, I came up alongside him. And elbowed him hard in the ribs.

The ref's whistle shrilled.

"Technical foul on number 11, Mickey "Spider" McGhee!"

I froze. A technical foul is the worst one you can get. It means you're a rotten sport who doesn't play fair. I had no business elbowing that Dolphin. I knew it. And I also knew why I did it. I was jealous of Zack.

After we lost the game, Coach Duffy charged over to me before I was even off the floor. "What were you thinking out there?" he demanded.

"You think cheating is the way to get ahead? You think that's how to make starter some day?"

Ever since I'd made the team I'd wanted to be a starter like Zack, Tony, LaMar, Luis, and Sam Sherman. And now I'd probably blown any chance I ever had. "No, sir," I mumbled, staring at my feet. "I'm sorry. I really am. I won't do it again."

Coach scowled. "You got that right, McGhee," he barked. "You're sitting out the next game."

I couldn't believe my ears. We were playing the Wadsworth Wildcats next week. From what I'd heard, I was just the kind of player who could do serious damage to their standings. And now I was going to be sitting on the bench doing nothing. Miserably, I headed for the locker room.

Trish Riley saw me pass and left her friend Brittany. "Mickey McGhee," she stormed, grabbing my arm. "What's the matter with you? Why did you poke that guy with your elbow? You know that's not being a good sp ..."

I pulled my arm away and stalked off. This was getting stupid. It wasn't THAT big of a deal, I told myself. NBA guys got technical fouls all the time. It's just part of the game. But deep down I knew I was kidding myself. Being a bad sport sure wasn't loving my neighbor.

In the locker room neither Tony nor LaMar

said anything. Tony still had an ice pack on his shoulder. LaMar was busy putting new laces in his sneakers. Zack looked at me and shook his head like he still couldn't believe it. But he didn't say anything either. Only Sam Sherman spoke to me.

"Hey, Shrimpo, what was the deal out there? You cost us, you know."

I looked away and grabbed my gym bag. Sam didn't let up the whole time I changed. When I was done I slammed out of the locker room without saying anything to anybody. My parents were waiting by the door with Meggie.

"You OK, buddy?" Dad asked. I could tell by his face that he knew how awful I felt.

"I'm fine," I said shortly. But even Meggie knew better. Usually after a game she's all charged up. Today she didn't try to do cheers or tell me what she'd had to eat or anything.

We waited for Zack and then headed out to the parking lot. Mom gave my neck a quick squeeze, but didn't say anything. That's how my mom is though. She'll yell at me to clean up my room or not ride my bike across Wooster Street. But when it comes to stuff like being a good sport she lets me know how she feels by being nice to me. It made me feel worse than if she yelled.

At home she fixed baloney sandwiches and chicken noodle soup. I ate half of one sandwich and stirred my soup around. Zack talked to Meggie.

"You'd better hurry, Mickey," Mom said finally. "Mrs. Steffins is expecting you in five minutes."

I looked up at the clock shaped like a cat and sighed. I'd forgotten all about babysitting Dulcie. I glanced at Zack. He was staring into his bowl like he was trying to see the blue flower pattern under the soup. I was kind of hoping he might change his mind and come with me. I'd rather have Chinese Water Torture than go over to the Steffins' house alone. But I'd promised. And I couldn't afford to rack up any more black marks for the day.

"OK, I'm going," I mumbled. I stood up and took my dishes over to the sink. "See you guys later," I said, standing by the door. I grabbed my jacket off the peg by the basement steps and waited to see what Zack would do.

"Bye, Mickey," Mom and Meggie said together.

Zack fixed himself another baloney sandwich.

8

Funny Business

A pink and purple bike whizzed by as I came down the driveway.

"Hi, Trish!" I called.

She kept on going and didn't look back. At the sidewalk I stopped and stared up the street after her. I couldn't believe it. Trish Riley wouldn't miss a chance to talk to me if it meant walking on rusty nails. Maybe she hadn't seen me.

I waited at the curb for a car to pass. It's not like I care about talking to her or anything. It's just that I hate being ignored. When the car was gone I started to cross. Maybe she was coming right back, I decided. Yeah, that was it. She hadn't seen me and she was coming right back. I stepped up on the curb and waited.

Sure enough, the pink and purple bike zipped around the corner. She slowed down when she saw me.

"Hi, ya, Trish!" I yelled.

Trish tugged on the brim of her baseball cap and glared. I moved into the middle of the sidewalk and waited for her to stop. She tried to swerve around me. I jumped in her path.

"Stop it, Mickey McGhee!" she screamed "What's the matter with you? You're acting like a big dumb bully!" She hopped off the pedals of her bike and almost crashed it in the grass.

Whaaaaat? How could the shortest kid in the whole fourth grade be a bully? Was the sun still in the sky? Do trees have roots? Do cats have whiskers? Or has the whole world gone crazy?

"I'm not a ..."

"Oh, yes, you are!" she stormed. "First you hit the Dolphins' ball when it was already in the air. Then you poked that guy in the ribs. And now you won't let me ride my bike on a public side-walk!"

"Wait a second!" I hollered. "That was a game. You have to be tough if you want to win at basketball. NBA guys get technicals all the time. And right now I was only trying to talk to you, for Pete's sake!"

Trish tugged on the brim of her cap again. "You can call it whatever you want, Mickey McGhee," she said. "But I call it being a bully. Now, get out of my way!"

She wheeled her bike around me, stood up on the pedals and pushed off toward home. I stood in front of my house with my mouth hanging open. OK, so I made a couple bad moves in the game. I admit it. But did I deserve all this? I kicked a rock out of my path and stalked across the street. Even before I got to the porch of the old Palmer place, Dulcie opened the front door.

"We're having a tea party," she announced. "And you're the waiter."

I groaned. Out loud. I couldn't help it. It was like it was "Beat Up Mickey Day" and everybody was invited.

Dulcie made me wear a red and white checked apron that said *Bon Appetit* on the front. All I can say is, whoever made it sure doesn't know English. I know for a fact that "appetite" was spelled wrong. And what kind of word is "Bon"? But I put it on and poured tea into a cup so small it wouldn't hold half a melted Popsicle.

"I want you to be a SINGING waiter," Dulcie said when I was done. She helped herself to a cookie. It was bigger than the plastic plate she put it on.

"I don't know how to be a singing waiter," I said, looking at the clock. It had been only ten minutes since her mother went down the basement to sort through boxes. "What would I sing?"

Dulcie looked up at me from under the roses hanging off her floppy pink hat. "How would I know?" she asked. "I'm only this many." Four empty fingers of a huge green glove flapped in the air.

I thought about what a waiter could sing. I thought about Trish calling me a bully. I thought about the technical. I thought about Zack going to Sam's party without me.

"Hurry UP!" Dulcie demanded.

"La, la, la-la-la-la-la-la-la-la-la-la, LA, LA!" I sang, making up the tune as I went. I swooped her plate away and twirled in a circle. "La, la, la-la-la-la-la-la-la-la-la-la-la-la-la-la, LA!"

Dulcie giggled. "That's good, Mickey!" she cried. "Do it some more!"

I grinned and sang louder. "LA! LA! La-la-la-la-la-la-la-la-la-la-la-la-la-la! LA!" The more I sang, the more I started getting into it. I twirled and danced and swooped dishes on and off the table. By the time I finished, Dulcie and I were both laughing so hard we were bent over double. And then—*zap!*—faster than a flicker I thought of something.

"Eureka!" I cried, slapping my forehead.

"My eka?" Dulcie asked, frowning. "What's 'my eka,' Mickey?"

I laughed. "Nothing. Never mind. Just eat your cookie."

I sat down at the elf-sized table in the corner of

her room and grabbed a chocolate chip cookie. I was so excited I could hardly sit still long enough to chew. It was so clear what was wrong. Things were going bad because I'd been trying to act like a tough guy. Dulcie had shown me a whole new way to be the neighbor everybody *had* to love.

I came home $5 richer and a whole lot happier. Zack was on the phone in the kitchen when I walked through the door.

"Yeah, he knows," he was saying into the phone. He looked up, saw me, and turned away. "Listen, I can't talk right now," he said. "I'll catch up with you Monday."

I took off my jacket and hung it on the peg. He'd been talking about me. I could feel it like— like—well, like a hard poke in the ribs.

"Hi," I said, as he hung up the phone. "What's up?"

"Nothin' much," Zack answered. He didn't look at me.

Muggsy and Piston tore into the kitchen. At least *they* were happy to see me. I reached down to pet them and got a bath. Two wet tongues covered every inch of my face. "Eeeeeew!" I cried, cleaning the dog germs off with my sleeve. Then I remembered my bright new idea.

"Hey, Zack," I said. "Knock. Knock."

"Huh?" Zack looked startled. I guess I can't

blame him. I'm not usually a big joke teller.

"Knock, KNOCK," I repeated.

"Uh, OK. Who's there?" he asked. He was still looking at me like I'd fallen on my head during the game.

"Alaska."

"Alaska, who?" he asked.

I grinned and answered in a funny voice like a stand-up comic. "Alaska ya again—open the door already!"

Zack didn't laugh.

"Get it?" I asked. "Alaska? I'll ask ya?" I laughed way harder than the joke was worth.

"Ha-ha. Very funny," Zack said. "It's a million years old, Mick." He picked up his basketball book from the counter and went into the living room.

I followed him. "You should have seen me over at Dulcie's," I said, trying again. "She wanted me to be a singing waiter, so I started making up this tune and twirlin' around. It cracked her up." I showed him how I'd swooped the dishes on and off the table. "Funny, huh?"

Zack shrugged. "Yeah, sure," he said. It was easy to see he really didn't think so. He flopped down on the couch and opened his book.

I sat in the chair across from him and watched him read. My new idea wasn't working. Being a clown wasn't any better than being a tough guy.

"Hey," I said when I couldn't stand the quiet any more. "I got another $5 today. I don't think there will be many more jobs though. Mrs. Steffins is pretty much done putting stuff away. But it gives us $20." I threw out the word "us" like a fisherman throws a line in the water.

Zack closed his book. "Mick, I need to talk to you about the money," he said.

I frowned. He'd said *the* money. Not *our* money. Not even *your* money. But *the* money. "What about it?" I asked. All of a sudden I felt alert. Like a cat who'd just spotted a chipmunk.

"Well, the thing is," Zack began. He traced the picture on the cover of his book with his finger. He wouldn't look at me. "I sorta need my share."

What did he mean HIS share? *I'm* the one who'd done most of the babysitting. The first day he'd quit as soon as his dad left. And today he didn't even go at all. "For what?" I asked.

Zack kept running his finger over the outline of the picture. "Well, uh—I gotta buy something for Sam's birthday," he mumbled.

It was true then. He was going to the party. I tried to do some mental math, but I couldn't. I was too upset. "Your share isn't much," I said. My voice was as frosty as a Sno-Kone. "You were only there a little while Sunday. And you didn't even go today."

Zack nodded. "I know," he agreed. "But I should get half of the $10 from the night she got lost. That's $5. And half of my half from Sunday. That's $1.25. You owe me $6.25, Mick."

My head reeled. It was probably true. Zack's way better at math than I am. I didn't know what $6.25 from $20 came to. But I did know this:

The Globetrotters were history. And Zack Zeno was not my best friend anymore.

9

Fun-raising

"I don't see what you're so mad about," Zack said. "You're the one who told me to go ahead and go to the party."

It was true. I did say that. But a good best friend wouldn't do it. And if he did, he sure wouldn't take a lot of the Globetrotter money with him.

I got up and walked over to the window. Trish whizzed by on her bike, but didn't look at my house.

"Didn't you tell me to go ahead and go?" Zack demanded. "*Didn't* you? Well, I can't very well go without taking a present, can I? In case you haven't noticed, my dad isn't here to give me any money for one."

I felt my muscles tighten. There it was again. Poor Zack with no Dad. Was I going to have to listen to that for four whole months? "I don't care whether you go to the party or not," I lied. "What I care about is my tickets. Now thanks to YOU I can't go to the Globetrotters at all. No way can I make up that money in time."

There was a long silence. Then Zack let out a huge sigh and said, "Mick, I hate to tell you this, but it really doesn't matter. You couldn't go anyway. The tickets are all sold out."

I whipped around and stared at him. "What are you talking about? How do you know? You don't know! You're just saying that."

Zack rubbed both hands over his face and let out another sigh. "LaMar told me," he said miserably. "His parents tried to get some. He told me today in the locker room. I'm really sorry, Mick, but it's the truth."

I didn't answer. It was so unfair. It was the most unfair thing I'd ever heard. Even more unfair than having to make up extra snow days at school. I'd worked so hard. Playing circus train. And nearly losing Dulcie. And being a singing waiter. And for what? For nothing, that's what!

"Look, I just won't go," Zack offered. "It's not worth having a fight over. It's just that your mom said it would be OK. And you said you didn't mind."

A rusty, beat-up car with a loud muffler went by. I watched as black smoke poured out of the tailpipe and floated in the air. In my head Mom's voice reminded me that God wants me to love my neighbor. I took a deep breath, let it out slowly, and watched as it fogged the glass. I opened my mouth to tell Zack to go ahead and go. But my mouth seemed to want to decide things for itself.

"OK, that's it. I'm not going," Zack said, standing up. "I'm calling Sam right now." He walked into the kitchen and picked up the phone.

I listened as he punched in the first three numbers. *Stop him*, a little voice inside me whispered. He punched in two more numbers. *Whatever you did for one of the least of these brothers of Mine, you did for Me.* These words flashed through my brain clearer than if they'd been written in the fog on the window. Would I try to stop Jesus from going to see the Globetrotters if *He* got an invitation? No way, man! No WAY! Then why was it OK to do it to Zack? The thought was so awesome, it about knocked me over.

"Wait!" I hollered, running into the kitchen. I pressed down the button that hangs up the call. "Don't," I said to Zack. "I want you to go to the party."

"You do?" His eyes bugged out like he couldn't believe it.

"Well, not really," I admitted. "But I WANT to want to."

Zack grinned. "I know what you mean, Mick," he said. "Thanks."

I had done the right thing. I knew it. And I felt

weak with relief. But that didn't mean I wanted to stick around and talk about it. Or listen to Zack talk about it. All I wanted was to be in my own room with my own dog by my own self. And that's just what I did. I called Muggsy and he and I went upstairs and closed the door of my room. Then we climbed into the bottom bunk and fell asleep. The day had worn us out.

The next thing I knew Mom was at the bottom of the stairs calling, "Mickey! Dinner!"

I sat up and blinked my eyes. Somehow it had started to get dark outside. It was hard to believe that today was still the same day as that horrible game. The same day I'd played singing waiter for Dulcie. The same day I'd stopped Zack from calling Sam.

"Coming, Mom!" I yelled. Muggsy leaped off my bed and ran to the door, his tail waving like a flag in a windstorm.

"Come on, boy," I said. "Let's go eat."

I was even sort of hungry. That is, until I saw what we were having. Fish. I hate fish. Especially white fish that doesn't have crunchy stuff on it. Worse yet, we were having lima beans to go with it. I hate plain white fish, but I REALLY hate lima beans. You get a big bunch of lima beans in your mouth and they taste like dry green paste. And then the skins fall off the beans and get stuck to your teeth. Yeeeeeech!

To make it worse, it was Meggie's turn to say grace. It always takes her three million years because she gets grace mixed up with bedtime prayers. She asked God to bless everybody from each of us to Dulcie's dog, Taco, and the mailman.

When she was done, Mom served me a plate of food. Then she said to Zack, "When do you want to shop for a birthday present for Sam?"

I stared down at my white fish and green lima beans and felt sorry for myself. Zack muttered, "Anytime."

"How about Monday afternoon after school?" Mom asked dishing up lima beans for Meggie. "We can go to Kmart. Meggie needs new tennies and Mickey could use some underwear."

Underwear. Zack gets to shop for something fun. Meggie gets new shoes. And I get *underwear*. I poked at my fish and stabbed a lima bean with my fork.

"I guess Monday would be OK. That OK with you, Mick?" Zack asked.

I could see he was trying to be nice. I tried to be nice back. "Sure," I said.

"Good! Then it's settled," Mom said brightly. "It'll be fun. We'll get some fresh popcorn and you guys can have it for a snack later. What would you say to that?"

I knew Mom was trying. She knows I love that buttery, salty popcorn you can't make at home, no matter what you do. But I was still the most miserable kid on the planet.

Dad started to say something about the Kent State game being on TV tonight. The doorbell cut him off.

"Mickey, will you go see who that is?" Mom asked. "Be sure to put the porch light on and look out first," she added. She tells me that every single time I answer the door at night.

I shoved back my chair and went to the front door. I flipped on the light and pushed back the curtain. A man was standing on the porch. I'd seen him somewhere before, but I wasn't sure where. I opened the door and waited for him to say something.

"You must be Mickey," he said, looking me over. "I'm Jim Steffins, Dulcie's dad."

My heart speeded up. He'd been out of town. Could he just have gotten home and heard about me and Zack almost losing his kid? "Oh. Uh. I mean hi," I said. My face turned redder than spaghetti sauce.

"Mind if I come in?" he asked. "I have something I want to talk to you about."

I gulped and opened the door. He came into

the living room. Through the doorway he could see back into the kitchen. "Oh my. You're having dinner. I'm sorry," he said when he saw everybody sitting at the table. "I can come back later."

Mom scraped back her chair and rushed into the living room. "No, no, of course you won't!" she called. "Come in, Jim, please. What can we do for you?"

Mr. Steffins is a tall, skinny man with ears like jug handles. He ducked his head and stuffed his hands into his coat pockets. "Well, the thing is," he said. "I was talking to my daughter today and she told me some interesting things about Mickey."

My heart raced like a V-8 engine. Had I done anything else besides almost losing the only child he had? I didn't think so. But Dulcie could probably think of something.

"It seems she likes you," he said, flashing me a grin. I must have looked surprised because he shrugged and sort of laughed. "Anyway, her mom and I are going to be busy Thursday night and we need somebody to keep an eye on her."

Thursday night. The night of the big Globetrotter's game. Staying home was bad enough. But staying home and babysitting was a million times worse. I stared at the floor and didn't say anything. If only he had called on the phone, it would have been easy to say no.

"Mickey would be happy to help, wouldn't you, honey?" Mom said, before I could think of an excuse.

I looked up. Mr. Steffins caught my eye and laughed that same funny laugh as before. Like he somehow understood what I was feeling. "So, is it a deal?" he asked me.

I nodded. It really WAS "Beat Up Mickey Day!"

"Well, that's great then!" He reached out a long, bony hand and ruffled my hair. "I really appreciate this, buddy. My wife and I both are working on this fund-raiser and Dulcie keeps pestering us to take her. The only way we could is if …"

"F-f-f-fund-raiser?" I stammered. I didn't get it. Was I supposed to watch Dulcie somewhere else? My mind flashed to basketball practice and how I'd nearly lost her.

Mr. Steffins laughed. A real laugh this time. Loud and long. He said, "Mickey, you and Dulcie are going to the Harlem Globetrotters game."

10

Short-shirted

When I got back to the table, Zack was grinning so wide I thought his face would crack. "I heard," he said. "It's great, Mick!"

Already my mind had made two lists. Plus Side: I was going to the game for free. Minus Side: I was going with a four-year-old.

"I guess so," I mumbled.

"OK, so maybe it's a little weird. But it sure beats not going at all. Right?" he insisted.

"Right," I said. I wasn't sure whether I really believed it though.

I still didn't know on Monday when we went to Kmart to get Sam's gift. All weekend I had been dreading the shopping trip. But when we got there Zack started acting so weird I completely forgot about myself.

"What's wrong with you?" I asked after he'd raced down the toy aisle three times.

Zack sighed and slumped against a shelf full of Star Wars stuff. "I—I don't know what to get," he said. "Sam's so rich and I only have $6 and enough left over for tax. What can I buy for that?"

I couldn't believe it. Zack got invited to the party. But he felt as stupid around Sam as I did! Lately I'd thought they were getting to be buddies. At least sort of. And now Zack felt weird about getting a gift because Sam was rich and he wasn't.

"I know what you can get," I said, leading him to the aisle with the yo-yos. At our school yo-yos are hotter than the lit end of a firecracker. I'd seen a huge one with a wild spiral design. It was painted practically every color ever invented.

"Look," I said taking it off its hook. "This thing is waaaaay COOL. It looks like a giant sucker. You get it really moving and it'll boggle your eyes."

Zack wrinkled up his forehead. "It's cool all right," he agreed. "But do you think it's enough? I mean Sam is used to getting everything he wants."

"So what? This is a great gift." Something I learned at church whizzed through my mind. "Look at it this way," I argued. "You're kinda like that widow in the Bible. She was poor, but she gave away everything she had. The rich people gave a lot, but it was really only a little bit because they had tons of money left over. See? You're just like her. I say get the yo-yo and don't sweat it."

Zack grinned and tossed the yo-yo in the cart. "Thanks, Mick," he said.

On Thursday night I was already gone when Sam's mom came to pick up Zack. Dulcie's parents had to be at the high school early. As soon as we pulled into the parking lot, I spotted the red, white, and blue bus that said "Harlem Globetrotters" on the side.

"Wow!" I breathed as we walked past it. I brushed my shoulder against the side just to be able to say I'd touched it.

Already people were starting to pour through the doors. Mr. Steffins handed in tickets for Dulcie and me and took us into the gym. "Those were VIP passes," he told me as he led us to our seats. "OK, here you go." He waved us into the front row. "Stay here and I'll get you a couple of programs. OK?"

I was speechless. We were going to be sitting courtside!

"Watch me dance, Mickey," Dulcie said as soon as her dad was gone. She spun around in a circle and kicked one leg out to the side. "See? I'm like a football girl."

"Huh?" All I could think about was how little space there was going to be between me and Reggie the Regulator. "What's a football girl?"

Dulcie put her hands on her hips and brought

her face up close to mine. "You KNOW it's a dancing girl at the football game," she said glaring at me. "YOU'RE JUST NOT PAYING ATTENTION! AND THAT'S BEING A BAD BABYSITTER!"

She was right. I wasn't paying attention. Sam and his guests had just walked in the door. I spotted Trish's purple baseball cap and Zack's dark hair. Dulcie followed my gaze.

"HI, ZACK!" she screeched. "ME AND MICKEY ARE OVER HERE!"

Eight heads swiveled to look at us. Zack waved. So did Tony, LaMar, and Luis. Even Trish sort of halfway waved. I think she forgot for a minute that she was mad at me. Only Sam didn't wave. When he saw me sitting in a VIP seat, his mouth dropped open. But not for long. He snapped it shut and pretended to open an imaginary umbrella. I couldn't help it. My face turned redder than the stripes on the Globetrotters' shorts.

I couldn't look at him leading the way up the steps to the bleachers. I knew he was making fun of me. When Mr. Steffins came back with the programs I grabbed mine and opened it. I wanted to find Reggie the Regulator. I leafed through the big shiny pages and stopped cold. The Globetrotters had hired a brand new player named Jimmy "Pee Wee" Henry. He was only

5'3", shorter even than Muggsy Bogues and Earl Boykins!

"Look, Dulcie," I said, pointing to his picture. "Isn't he great? He's short like me."

Dulcie grabbed the picture and stared at it. "Yes, he's neat," she said. "But he's not like you, Mickey. He has big muscles. And he's a GOOD basketball player."

I grabbed the program back. I wanted to say that I would have muscles too when I was out of college. And that I was already a good basketball player. But just then Globie, the mascot, walked out on the floor waving at the crowd. Dulcie squealed and hopped up and down in her seat. I watched in a daze as Globie danced with a couple of moms. He was funny, but I wanted to see the Globetrotters so bad it was torture to sit still. When the music changed to "Sweet Georgia Brown," I caught my breath. The Globetrotter theme song! And then, suddenly, there they were! Right in front of me dribbling their red, white, and blue basketballs.

"LOOK, MICKEY! SEE THE LITTLE PEE-WEE!" Dulcie screeched in my ear.

Number 57, Jimmy Henry, turned around and flashed her a grin. Prickles of pleasure played tag on my arms. I was so excited I almost couldn't breathe right. Zack, Sam, and the rest of the party guests might as well have been in Tibet after that. It wasn't until halftime that I turned around and craned my neck to find them.

"MICKEY, THAT BIG MAN IS LOOKING AT YOU!" Dulcie bellowed in my ear as I scanned the rows. She grabbed my arm and yanked it hard.

I turned around and went face-to-kneecap with a giant. A giant so tall he made old George from the Brunswick Blue Dolphins look like a Keebler cookie elf. It was number 32, Paul "Showtime" Gaffney. He wanted me to come out on the floor and shoot baskets!

"DO IT, MICKEY!" Dulcie screamed. "DO IT!"

Somehow I stood up and walked out onto the court. It was unreal. Not possible. Unbelievable. Any minute I would hear the sound of Mom dragging the door of my room across the carpet and calling, "Time to get up, Mickey!" But it didn't happen. No door thud. No Mom. No wake-up call. Just me out on the court shooting from the free throw line!

One! A success!

Two! Another success!

Three! The ball rolled on the rim, wobbled— and sank. Rack up another winner!

The crowd went crazy.

"What's your name?" Showtime asked me after

I sank the third one.

"M-M-Mickey McGhee," I stammered.

"Well, M-M-Mickey McGhee, it looks like you won yourself the official Globetrotter's T-shirt," Showtime hollered, waving a red, white, and blue shirt.

A sea of Globetrotters closed in around me. Somebody jerked my old T-shirt over my head. I waited for the quick darkness of the new one to fall over my face, but it didn't. Instead the sea parted and the Globetrotters backed up. I blinked in the harsh glare of the spotlight and looked around. My bony shoulders, stick arms, and skinny chest were right out there on display. I was standing alone in the middle of the floor with no shirt on! Compared to my face, I figured the Exit sign by the door must look pale pink.

But then, almost as fast as they'd left, the Globetrotters crowded around me again. The new shirt popped over my head. I struggled to push my arms through the sleeves. Reggie the Regulator helped on one side and Pee Wee on the other. They just got the shirt on me when a tiny torpedo with wild fuzzy hair crashed through their knees.

"YOU BAD GLOBETROTTERS!" she yelled, shoving at their legs. "Mickey is MY babysitter! AND I DON'T THINK YOU SHOULD TAKE

HIS CLOTHES OFF!"

The crowd howled and stamped their feet. The Globetrotters moved away, leaving me and Dulcie alone in the spotlight. The players were laughing so hard they were holding their sides. I traded glances with Reggie the Regulator and cracked up. I laughed until tears dripped out of the sides of my eyes.

Through the blur I spotted Trish's purple baseball cap way up high in the stands. She was waving both arms in the air and mouthing my name. So were Tony, Luis, and LaMar. My eyes moved across the row in search of Zack. I found him standing next to Sam yelling his head off. When he saw that I'd seen him he flashed me the OK sign. I flashed it back.

Then I looked down at Dulcie. She was standing in the spotlight with her hands on her hips still glaring at the Globetrotters. One look into those fierce blue eyes and—wham!—it hit me like a freight train. I WAS the neighbor somebody wanted to love! And I had been all along. I just hadn't been paying attention.

A bouncy rock n' roll song poured through the gym. Its beat pulsed in my brain and shot through my muscles. I grabbed Dulcie's hand and twirled her around.

"Come on, Dulcie, shake it," I told her. "Be a

football girl!"

For half a second she looked surprised. Then she broke into a huge grin and shouted, "WATCH ME, MICKEY!"

She snapped her fingers, tossed her fuzzy head, and pranced like a pony. Dulcie only danced in the warm spotlight for a few seconds. But I watched her like a coach watches his star player.

Sixth Man Switch

One Extra-Large Miracle to Go

ATTENTION BOYS!
Basketball Teams Now Forming
Grades 4–6
Have Fun!
Make Friends!
Get Fit!

"Hey, look!" my best friend Zack Zeno shouted, pointing to the sign on the red brick wall of the city pool house. "Just what we've been waiting for!"

I shoved a weird black rock I'd found on the ground into the side pocket of my jeans and went over to check it out.

"Tryouts are Saturday morning," I read. "We're in, buddy!" I slapped him a high five and we pretended to do a jump shot.

Zack and I are total basketball freaks. Someday we're going to be high school hotshots. Then college all-stars. Then NBA pros. We've got it all planned. But until now we figured we'd have to wait until sixth grade to play on a real team.

"Hey!" somebody hollered from the parking lot next to the pool house.

It brought our feet down hard on the sidewalk. Every time I hear that voice I feel like I just got punched in the stomach. I could be at a real live Bull's game and the sound of that know-it-all tone would spoil the whole thing. Michael Jordan could sink a winning three-pointer and I'd be feeling sicker than the winner of a pie-eating contest.

"Hey, Sam!" I hollered back. I always pretend like Sam Sherman doesn't get to me. But it's getting harder and harder to do. Not only does he make my life miserable, but he also gets everything he wants. He even gets everything *I* want, which right now includes a dog and being tall enough to play center.

I know the last one will never happen, but I might actually get a dog someday. At least that's what my mom says. Trouble is, she's been saying it for two years already and "someday" is no closer than it ever was.

"You guys trying out for the team?" Sam asked. He came toward us, dribbling what looked like a brand new basketball. His huge black Lab, Zorro, pranced along beside him sporting a bright red collar.

"We might," Zack said.

"Yeah, we might," I agreed.

Sam dribbled the ball under his leg and lost control of it. It rolled off the sidewalk into the grass.

Zack and I grinned as he ran after it.

Sam picked up the ball and walked the rest of the way to the pool house. "You'd better get in some serious practice then," he warned. "Most of the guys who have a chance to make the team were at basketball camp this summer."

My heart sank. Well, not really. That's just a thing people say when they're upset. But if hearts *could* sink, mine would have ended up somewhere around my ankles. Sam was right. At the end of last year, a player from the local pro team came to our school and passed out flyers about the camp. Everyone who was serious about basketball signed up. Except for Zack and me. Basketball camp cost more than $100. Even without asking, we knew our parents couldn't afford it.

"We don't need basketball camp," I said now, heading toward my bike. "We're naturals."

"Naturals!" Sam scoffed. He laughed so hard he doubled up over the ball. "When's the last time you looked in the mirror, McGhee?" he asked me. "You're a little shrimp."

I picked up my bike from the ground where I'd crashed it and jumped on. Already I could feel my ears burning. It was like Sam Sherman held a remote control. All he had to do was press a button, and I turned as red as a sunburn. I'm the shortest boy in the fourth grade. Most of the *girls* are even taller than I am.

"Size doesn't matter," Zack said loyally, jumping on his bike too. "Mickey's got speed."

I didn't say anything. Sam was showing off his crossover dribble. It was so fast and clean, you could set it to music. He'd sure learned a lot at that basketball camp.

Zorro barked and ran in little circles as the ball bounced across the concrete. Usually I like to watch Zorro, but not today. I rode off toward home with Zack behind me. We didn't talk until we crossed the street and were safely in our own neighborhood. Then he rode up alongside me.

"Don't let him get to you," he said. "We're in. We're in!"

"I know," I agreed. But I wasn't so sure anymore.

At my house, I turned onto the bumpy gravel driveway and Zack followed. Our old ten-speeds rattled like two jars of marbles. We squeezed our handbrakes and came to a stop, sending the gravel flying.

"Want to do a little one-on-one before supper?" Zack asked.

"OK." I dropped my bike and got my basketball from the garage. I'd told my mom I'd clean my room after school, but maybe if I didn't go into the house, she'd forget for awhile.

I bounced the ball a few times on the pad by the side door of the house. The thud, thud, thud sound it made slapping against the fresh concrete made my muscles unclench. My dad and I had just poured that pad two weeks ago. We built the frame and everything. When the cement was ready, Dad mounted a metal pole in the ground to hold the basket. Later Zack and I painted it black. Nobody could even tell it used to be a city lightpole we got for free.

I tossed the ball to Zack and he pivoted wildly in all directions, trying to freak me out.

"Dee-fense! Dee-fense!" I shouted, trying to block with my arms.

Zack laughed and shot over my head. The ball hit the rim and bounced off. We both scrambled for it.

"Hi, Mickey!"

I froze, both hands on the ball. There's only one other voice besides Sam Sherman's that can stop me cold, and this was it. I let go of the ball and straightened up.

"Hi, Trish," I said.

Trish Riley lives down the street and sits in front of me in Mrs. Clay's class. It's totally embarrassing to admit this, but she has a monster crush on me. I hate it. Neither Zack nor I want to get involved with girls. At least not until we're 27. Maybe even 30!

She pulled the brim of the baseball cap she always wears down over her forehead and smiled. "You're really good, Mickey. I bet you make the team."

Zack pretended like he was practicing his speed dribble. But I could see his shoulders shaking up and down from laughing. Good? What did Trish Riley know about good? I'd just let Zack complete a throw that should have gone in easy.

"Thanks." I turned back to Zack, but Trish made no move to leave.

"I guess you heard about Sam Sherman," she said.

"What about him?" I could feel my muscles tensing up again.

Now that she had my attention, Trish walked up the driveway. "Last Saturday he landed a pair of baskets in front of 2000 people at an exhibition game."

"Huh?" Suddenly I was all ears.

She nodded. "It's true. He went up to State to see his brother play. His brother's a big star at the university, you know."

Zack stopped dribbling and came over. "Sam Sherman didn't play at any State game," he said. "No way. No way!" But you could tell he wasn't sure.

Now that she had Zack's attention too, Trish continued her story. "Yes, he did," she said, yanking on her baseball cap again. That's something she does whenever she talks to me. "At halftime they toss T-shirts into the crowd. If you catch one, you get to go down on the floor and shoot. Sam grabbed one, raced down there and shot two baskets right in a row. No misses."

Zack and I exchanged glances. I knew he was thinking the same thing I was. *How thrilling it would be to hear the crowd roaring its approval, especially for a fourth grader.*

"Oh yeah? So what?" I said, reaching down for the ball Zack had left on the ground.

Trish saw she was losing us. "He won a real prize too," she added. "Got a whole wad of coupons for free food. Burgers, shakes, fries, all kind of free stuff."

We let that sink in. Rarely did we get to eat fast food. I couldn't even remember when I'd last wrapped my mouth around a bacon cheeseburger. But that wasn't the important part. The big thing was Sam Sherman out on the court shooting baskets at a college game.

Zack and I looked at each other again. We didn't even have to say it.

We were dead.

Behind me a window squeaked open on the side of the house. "Mickey McGhee! You get in here and clean your room this minute!" my mom shouted.

Red crawled up my neck and stained my face like cherry Kool-Aid. "I gotta go," I mumbled.

I picked up my bike, tossed the basketball in the dented wire basket and wheeled the bike up the driveway to the garage. "See ya, Zack!" I called. I didn't say good-bye to Trish. It's not that I was trying to be rude or anything. I just didn't want her getting any more ideas than she already had.

Our garage is only big enough for one car. So I always have to make sure to get my bike tight against the wall so my dad doesn't drive his pickup into it. I did that, then walked back toward the house.

In my head I could hear the college band playing "Hang On Sloopy" during halftime. I could smell the nachos and taste the icy blast of freshly poured pop. But mostly, I could feel the excitement crackling like wrapping paper around an Easter basket, as Sam Sherman strutted his stuff on the wide, polished floor.

It made me groan right out loud. We were only kidding ourselves. For Zack Zeno and Mickey McGhee to land a spot on the basketball team it was going to take a miracle!

On the scale of, say, the loaves and the fishes. Or the wedding feast of Cana.

In other words, a real doozy!

Only Jesus could pull off something that big!

Sixth Man Switch

"It made me groan right out loud. We were kidding ourselves. It was going to take a miracle for Zack Zeno and Mickey McGhee to land a spot on the basketball team."

Fourth-grader Mickey McGhee and his best friend, Zack Zeno, eat, sleep, and breathe basketball. When the city announces a basketball league for their age group, they are thrilled.

But Sam Sherman and his friends plan to try out as well; no doubt they will be using height and fast new moves to score important spots on the team. What chances do these two friends have against taller fellow athletes who trained at a pro basketball camp? A lot!

Spider McGhee and the Hoopla

"I'm looking for the little guard," said Dave Dawson from the Gazette. "Number 11. There he is! Hey kid, where'd you learn to play b-ball like that?"

When fourth-grader Mickey McGhee becomes the surprising basketball dynamo in the city league, everybody notices, including the media. Because of his speed and dexterity, he earns the nickname "Spider" and a following of fans.

But Mickey forgets something in all the media excitement and hype that nearly ruins it all. He learns the importance of friendship, forgiveness and unconditional love—especially God's love.

Zip Zero Zilch

"I knew Mom was right about God and love and all that. But right now I felt too crummy to listen. When was I going to get to be the neighbor everybody was supposed to love?"

Sam Sherman's game is hotter than ever! He just can't seem to miss! Since Mickey's plays aren't getting any attention at all, he decides to make some game adjustments. And he gets plenty of attention—just the wrong kind!

Through it all, Mickey learns that responsibility to God, his friends, family, and himself is more important than scoring points or winning games. Read along as Mickey puts his faith into action.

Muggsy Makes an Assist

"I laughed so hard I dropped Muggsy's leash and fell against the wall, holding my sides. Then I saw my dog fly around the corner so fast it looked like all four paws were off the ground. 'Muggggseeee!' I called, dashing down the hall."

If Mickey could eat, sleep, and drink basketball, he would. There is nothing he would rather do than play one game and think about the next one.

But as Mickey focuses more and more on his basketball game, he has less time to concentrate on other things—even his new dog Muggsy is left out in the cold. But Mickey discovers a need to balance his priorities and concentrate on the important stuff. Read on to discover what happens!